Michaël Escoffier
Amandine Piu

BEWARE
the monster!

annick press
toronto + berkeley

WARNING!
THIS BOOK CONTAINS A MONSTER WITH A
GREAT BIG APPETITE!

Not here.
That's a cow.

AH, THERE HE IS!

WELL, YES, HE DOES LOOK PRETTY SMALL.
BUT THAT'S BECAUSE
HE'S **FAR AWAY**.

BE VERY QUIET,
OR YOU'LL WAKE HIM!

DRAT, YOU WOKE HIM UP!
WAIT – WHAT IS HE DOING?

OH MY GOSH — HE ATE ALL THE APPLES!
YOU'RE LUCKY HE HASN'T NOTICED YOU.

LOOK, HE ATE ALL THE LEAVES!

I THINK YOU'D BETTER HIDE.

OH NO, HE ATE ALL THE TREES!

GET DOWN, QUICK!

WAIT A MINUTE . . . .

WHERE ARE THE COWS?

DON'T TELL ME . . . .

YIKES, I THINK HE'S SPOTTED YOU.

YOU'VE GOT TO GET AWAY!

HERE HE COMES!

CLOSE
THE BOOK!

WELL, WHY DIDN'T YOU CLOSE IT?

NOW YOU'RE IN TROUBLE!

THERE'S NO ESCAPE!

Well, well.
A LITTLE
CHILD.

MY FAVORITE DISH.

COME HERE, DON'T BE
SCARED.

YOU LOOK
DELICIOUS.

I THINK I'M GOING TO...

I THINK I'M

Michaël Escoffier has written more than seventy picture books, which have been translated around the world. He lives in Lyon, France with his wife and two children.

Amandine Piu was born in 1982 in Sardinia, Italy, and studied visual arts in Lyon and later in Strasbourg, France.

© 2018 Michaël Escoffier (text)
© 2018 Amandine Piu (illustrations)

First published in France in 2017 by © Éditions Frimousse
Translation rights arranged through the VeroK Agency, Barcelona, Spain

Annick Press edition, 2018
Translated by Paula Ayer

Library and Archives Canada Cataloguing in Publication

Escoffier, Michaël, 1970-
[Plus gros que le ventre. English]
    Beware the monster / Michaël Escoffier ; illustrated by Amandine Piu ; translated by Paula Ayer.

Translation of: Plus gros que le ventre.
Issued in print and electronic formats.
ISBN 978-1-77321-022-3 (hardcover).--ISBN 978-1-77321-023-0 (softcover).--
ISBN 978-1-77321-024-7 (PDF)

    I. Piu, Amandine, 1982-, illustrator II Ayer, Paula, translator
III. Title. IV. Title: Plus gros que le ventre. English

PZ7.E742Be 2018   j843'.92   C2017-905602-6
                                               C2017-905603-4

Published in the U.S.A. by Annick Press (U.S.) Ltd.
Distributed in Canada by University of Toronto Press.
Distributed in the U.S.A. by Publishers Group West.

Printed in China   MAY 2 3 2018

www.annickpress.com
www.michaelescoffier.com
http://www.piupiu.fr/

Also available in e-book format. Please visit www.annickpress.com/ebooks.html for more details.